The Magic Dragonfly Earrings
Ivy Zephyr

Alyssa Brown

Copyright

Dedication

To Mom and Dad, who instead of discouraging my dreams, encouraged me to chase them, or use them as inspiration for my stories. Here I am about to do both.

Chapter 1

I couldn't take it anymore. I had to get away. I knew if I stayed one minute longer I'd lose it.

It'd been three hours since I'd made the decision to leave. Three hours of traveling along abandoned highways in search of a new life. Or a million dollars. Whichever came first. I drove north out of the familiar city across the huge golden gate bridge feeling a little lost as I stared at the road in front of me. The faster I drove through the misty morning air, the faster my mind raced about what I was going to do.

My name is Ivy Zephyr. For the past few months, I'd been preparing to be the new Mrs. Byron Chandler. My fiance had promised me a life full of prosperity with the money he was due to inherit. Even though I loved the man before the money, my friends and family still continually teased me of being a golddigger. I took it in stride. I was taller than most but had that easy movement of not being in a hurry to go anywhere. My brown hair was nice with natural highlights that my friends were always jealous of because I didn't have to manage it. I was always too quiet to be of any attention but we had a lot of fun as a couple. I still couldn't believe he threw it all away on someone else.

Everything had been perfect until just this morning. After coming back early from a cruise with my mom up north, I was excited to come home to finalize wedding preparations. As I entered the bedroom I found Byron asleep with another woman. Of course the jerk denied it, but the evidence was stacked against him.

After leaving to clear my head, I called my mom to explain what happened. But instead of supporting me, she told me I'd overreacted, and that what he did was perfectly normal. She told me to forgive and forget. That only made me angrier.

"Mother, I am leaving him. That is that. What he did was inexcusable."

"Just give it time dear. He'll come around before the wedding." Mom's voice was so breathy I wondered if she was even paying attention.

"How can you take his side? He's the one who messed up."

"Be patient darling. He's got plenty of money. Tell him to buy you a new gold necklace and everything will feel better, I promise. Oh, and while you're at it, make him pay for our next getaway, I could use another cruise in the near future."

My blood boiled. How could she be so calloused and nonchalant about this? Sure the guy was rich, but was that really the defining factor in our relationship? I didn't want it to be.

I told her I was leaving him and hung up before she could put in another word. After doing so, I packed up my basic necessities into my tiny car and drove, leaving my ex and his 5 karat diamond ring in my dust.

I did feel bad about hanging up on mom, but at the moment I was too angry. She had chosen my cheating fiance over her own daughter. I knew she wanted me to marry rich, but I refused to settle for a cheater.

As I drove on, I marveled at the continually changing scenery. After spending so long in the city, the fresh open air was exactly what I needed. I had no plan for where to go. I only knew that I wasn't going back. I'd quit my previous job as a museum curator in preparation for the wedding and a life of relaxation. College had drained most of my bank account, but I still had some left. I could last for a bit, but I would have to eventually find a job. And a place to stay. Oh and new friends. But one thing at a time. The first thing I had to do was find a gas station. Not only was my gas tank so low that the engine was running on fumes, but I was surviving on an empty stomach.

I drove for several more miles, and just as I was starting to get worried, I saw a sign for a small town just up ahead. The sign identified the town as Redwood Bluff. I'd never heard of Redwood Bluff, which confused me. But at that point, I was grateful to see some form of civilization.

When I finally made it to the town, I admitted that it was definitely a town. The small road and faded signs above the shops along mainstreet created an almost abandoned feel. Despite that, it was cozy. Several people were scattered as they walked up and down the streets without a care in the world. Quaint was the best way to describe it. I filled up my tank at a little gas station, but just as I was about to run in for a sandwich, I saw the sign for Mabel's Diner. I decided that after the morning I'd had, a hot meal was exactly what the doctor called for. My stomach growled in agreement.

The diner itself was small yet inviting; just like the rest of the town. A plump lady with graying hair walked up to me with a menu in one hand and a pad of paper in the other.

"Hey there sweetie, what can I get you started with today?" I couldn't place her accent, but regardless, her voice was warm and immediately caused my shoulders to relax. "Are you new to town? I don't think I've seen you in here before?"

I sat down and opened the menu to a wide selection of breakfast plates filled with pancakes, eggs, and hashbrowns.

"Are you interested in trying our pancakes with our new triple berry syrup? The syrup is made fresh right here, and it's a house favorite."

She spoke so fast that she literally gasped for air once she finished speaking. I tried not to laugh, I liked this lady already.

"Hi, I'm Ivy. I'm just passing through. I'll have one of whatever you just said right there, it sounded good."

The woman beamed with delight. "Wonderful to meet you Ivy. I'll get those pancakes going for you. And happy to help, my name is Mabel, and I'm the owner of this fine establishment. Just holler if you need anything."

Chapter 2

As I waited for my food, I looked around the diner. There was definitely a sense of community here. Everytime a customer walked in, a waitress greeted them by name. I'd grown up in the suburbs of San Francisco, so this was completely foreign to me. Regardless, the idea of living in an area small enough to know everyone by name was beginning to grow on me. Could I live here? I immediately pushed the thought out of my head. I had no place to stay and no job options. There were no museums to be seen, anywhere here. No one to take my resume. Besides, a part of me had simply planned to drive around, cool off, and eventually return home. I'd find a new apartment far away from the traitor, probably on the other side of the city would be far enough. But I still wanted to be close enough to visit my mother once she accepted that I wasn't going back to Byron. She'd have to realize that I wasn't going to put up with him cheating and lying to me just so she could retire in luxury.

At that moment, Mabel returned with a large stack of golden pancakes drizzled in a deep crimson syrup. A side of bacon and eggs was a welcome surprise. I dug into the pancakes, and was met with a syrup that popped with the taste of fresh berries. I smiled at the memory of picking blackberries while camping last summer. Then my smile vanished when I remembered that it was shared with the man who got me here in the first place. I set down my fork for a moment as I fought back tears.

Mabel unfortunately happened to be watching my every move. "What's the problem, sugar? Are the pancakes not to your liking?"

I jerked my head up and a single tear fell down my face. I wiped it quickly as my face burned. Mabel set her coffee pot down and sat down in the chair across from me.

"No, not at all. The pancakes are perfect." I quickly reassured her and watched her shoulders relax a little. I sniffed softly. "I've just had a crazy morning."

"Care to talk about it?" Mabel's voice was now more firm than soothing.

I paused for a moment. Did I want to share my issues with this woman? But I had a lot on my mind, and I really did need to talk.

"I got home early this morning from a week-long trip, and found my fiance in bed with another woman." Mabel's face turned sour. "At first, I wanted to deny it, but I was so angry." I took a deep breath to calm down. "On a whim, I decided to leave him before he could give an explanation. I packed up as much of my stuff as I could and drove away. I was low on gas, so I stopped in this town. I realized that in the middle of everything that happened, I missed breakfast. Now here I am." I shrugged my shoulders and wiped the tears from my eyes. Mabel just sat there with a stoic expression on her face.

"Where will you go? Do you have family nearby to help you?"

I took a deep breath remembering my second fight of the day. The second fight turned my stomach to knots, and I felt a hard pang in my chest.

"I called my mother as soon as I found out. She told me to take a breath and forgive my ex. The man who cheated on me. She told me that it was bound to happen sooner or later. She thinks men are greedy pigs. That was when I snapped and hung up on her."

Now Mabel just looked sad. "Your mother sounds like a woman who has given up on love."

I shrugged. "Anyways, now I'm on a journey to begin anew. What defines anew I don't know. I thought a new change of scenery might do me some good. I've been in the city all my life, so maybe it was time?"

Mabel paused for a moment before speaking again. "Have you thought about a job at all?"

"Not really, I quit my job just a few weeks ago, so I'll have to start the hunt as soon as possible."

The older woman looked thoughtful. "Come to think of it, I am in need of hiring a new waitress. The last one just left for college on the other side of the country. If you'd like, I can offer you a job at least for today. I've found that keeping my hands busy tends to clear the mind a bit."

Before, I would've said no. I've never worked as a waitress before, and it felt beneath me. I saw people in diners who looked downtrodden after being on their feet for hours on end. Plus I wasn't in the mood to deal with crabby people on a daily basis. At least in the museum I could simply call security and tell them to escort troublemakers away. But Mabel seemed like a good person, and the idea of keeping my hands busy right now felt like a cheaper alternative to driving around all day. "Ok, if you need help, I can step in for a few hours. Maybe you're right. Maybe it'll help me get my mind off this morning."

Mabel had a calm expression on her face, but her brown eyes had a glow. "Of course dear. I will need help with the lunch rush especially, but feel free to stay as long as you need."

Chapter 3

Once I had an apron on, I helped with the front of the diner with the other waitresses. A young blonde named Lily showed me how to fill out and send orders to the kitchen, and Amy asked me to help with refilling coffee cups. I watched in awe as her dark, shoulder length curls swept across her shoulders as she glided around the diner. She did it with such precision and speed that she looked as if she was skating. During the lull, Amy's husband Tom showed me how he made pancakes and sandwiches for all the customers. He did it with the same amount of precision and speed as his wife. I couldn't imagine the amount of energy their kids would have.

LIly filled me in on the town during the afternoon lull. From the way she described the place, it was a small town that hasn't done much in 50 years. A few wine stores and galleries were opening up as people tried to cater to the touristy folks. But even with it, they hadn't had much progress in the tourist industry. A few years of bad luck building up with some forest fires, bad weather and weird rumors floating around weren't much help to their economy.

As soon as the last customer was served and the sign was closed, my heart sank. Even though my feet hurt from standing all day, there was a sense of belonging and purpose here that I didn't realize I'd missed. Even though I'd made more at the museum, it hadn't felt as meaningful. There, I'd felt the need to prove myself to be the best. But here, I felt a sense of family. And the new feeling of a job well done that I did with my own hands.

Mabel wiped her hands on her apron as she walked over to me.

"Well Ivy, I think that does it for today. Have you considered my offer?"

I took a deep breath, and spoke my mind.

"If it's ok with you Mabel, I would be interested in filling that open waitress spot. I don't have my resume right now, but if you can give me until tomorrow, I can get it printed and-"

Mabel held her hand up. "I don't think that's necessary. I saw you work today, and I think you'd make a good addition to the team. I will need your resume for legal reasons, yes, but I would be happy to offer you the job now."

My eyes filled with tears. But these weren't tears over the life I'd lost with Byron, but for the new life and second chance I'd just been given here.

I couldn't believe the generosity of this woman. Mabel seemed to be like the grandmother I'd never had. Not only had she offered me a job, but a small one person apartment above the diner just for me. The skeptical part of my brain felt it was too good to be true.

"This is incredible Mabel. But aren't you afraid I'm taking advantage of you? I could secretly be planning to rob you in your sleep tonight you know."

Mabel shrugged. "You could be. But I secretly doubt that. The good nature you showed today would have been impossible to fake. Besides, if you're planning on robbing anyone, there's a fancy Italian Bistro just down the street that makes double what I do. You'd be more successful there." The staircase is in the back and I take care of locking up every night. She tossed me a key that she had already prepared, and gave me a funny half smile as she walked around the counter back into her office.

I thought about that. Maybe it was just the cautious side of me that came from living in San Francisco. You could never be too careful in a big city. But the idea of a whole kitchen downstairs, and a little apartment to myself was beyond what I'd imagined. I made a quick sandwich before saying goodnight to Tom and heading up the stairs for the night. Trying to climb the stairs I realized it was a tight fit trying to get my sandwich and luggage up at once. The apartment was tiny but so warm and inviting. The place reminded me of the fancy tiny bed and breakfast that I never experienced but dreamed of staying in.

I considered calling Mom, but decided against it. If I was going to call, it would be better in the morning when my head was more clear. Instead, I decided to explore the town. It was almost eight, but the sun wasn't down yet. I figured a short evening stroll would be good tonight.

The streets were a little busier than this morning. The night air was noticeably cooler with the summer ending. I loved the sight of the various small businesses scattered all down the street. Each of the restaurants had their wide doors open as if beckoning people in. Several people had the same idea as me, and I saw families pushing strollers, and couples holding hands as they walked. My heart panged as I missed the idea of romantic dinners and evening strolls. I was so distracted by one couple hugging that I almost walked into a lamp post. Fortunately, someone grabbed my arm at the last minute.

"Woah lady, easy. Don't go adding to the percentage of people with bumps on their heads. It's a nasty number."

I blinked a few times and turned toward the husky voice. It belonged to a lanky man with sideswept brown hair and dark eyes to match. He reminded me of those funny tall cowboys in the old westerns that walked like they were falling. But I could tell he had some strength in his scrawny arms. I looked away for a moment and cleared my throat.

"Hi, sorry. Um, thanks for saving me from the pole." My face flushed with embarrassment at my distracted state. "What was your name again?"

Luckily, his smile was warm and sincere. "I'm Nolan Brooks, and don't worry, even if I told everyone about your making out with the lamp post, they wouldn't believe me. I'm not exactly the popular kid on the block." I couldn't decide whether to feel relieved or annoyed at this remark.

"Um, thanks. Anyway, I should get going."

"Wait, aren't you going to tell me your name?" His eyes looked innocent enough, but I couldn't decide how much I trusted this stranger.

"Ivy Zephyr."

He nodded in acknowledgment. "Well Ivy Zephyr, I don't believe I've seen you around here before."

"I just moved here." I hoped that if I kept my sentences short, he'd move along.

"Where to and where from?" This guy was definitely persistent. I gave a mental sigh.

"I moved from San Francisco. I just got offered a job at Mabel's diner, so I'll be in town for a bit."

Nolan's eyes lit up as he nodded. "Mabels is definitely the best breakfast place in town." He leaned in and paused for dramatic effect, but it was more awkward than anything. "Would it be embarrassing for you if I came to the diner, or would you be able to put up with my rugged good looks long enough to serve me a cup of coffee?" His grin was almost boyish, and it was hard not to smile back.

"I don't think that'll be an issue for me."

"That's what they all say about me," he said.

"Which part do they say? Obnoxious flirt or lame attempts? I can't decide."

That was my cue to leave, and I walked away before he could respond. I'd just gotten my heart broken this morning, and I was already flirting with a man. What was my problem? I was supposed to be crying at home with a pint of ice cream watching a movie, yet I was on the streets flirting with another man with no shame whatsoever.

Chapter 4

As I walked down Main Street, I marveled at all the little shops. Some restaurants, a few clothing boutiques, and even a couple of bookstores. I peeked into the Redwood Bluff Fix-It Shop, but almost ran away when I saw the man behind the counter. A red haired man scowled at me while polishing a shotgun. I didn't want to know who he was, or why he was holding a gun. As I tried to catch my breath, I passed a series of small stores that advertised various wine tasting tours for tourists. There were many of them but it didn't seem like any of them had much foot traffic at all. The bookstore across the street appeared to be in the same state of neglect.

The galleries were the oddest feature in the town. I made a right down one of the smaller streets, and found the entire street scattered with them. A few of the galleries looked to be local artists just trying to make a few bucks by selling the latest art trends coming out of the bay area. The three that I walked into had artwork that was so bright or surreal that I couldn't understand how they drew in tourists. The last one I entered was run by a skinny bald man that made my skin crawl. He introduced himself as Gregor and I was convinced he was going to stab me or poison me in my sleep. The little man kept hovering by, insisting that I needed a painting covered in demonic skulls to keep the grim reaper away. I nearly ran out of there, and tried to ignore the scowling redhead as I passed by the same shop once more.

As I made my way to the end of the small street, I was prepared to turn right to go back to the diner. But out of the left corner of my eye, I saw a small shop sign on the corner titled Thistle Treasures. The building itself looked more like a Victorian house than a shop, but the lights were on. The porch was small but it held a rickety rocking chair in the corner. The building was pale green with a gray roof and white accents. The faded white trim around the porch was in need of a touch up. It was completely different compared to the modern buildings and shops that surrounded it, which only sparked my curiosity as I stepped up the stairs and into the shop.

My first thought as I stepped into the little building was that it was crowded. Not with people, but with objects. Nearly every inch of the space was filled with it. But I didn't see any treasures, just stuff. The whole area was once a house, but it was filled to the brim with furniture, statues, and shelves piled high with books, jewelry, and knicknacks. But the longer I looked around, the more I saw there was a method to the madness. Different rows housed different items. A row for books, a row for furniture, eventually, I made my way to the other side of the room. That was when I realized I wasn't alone in the sea.

Behind a cash register sat a white haired lady in a pale pink sweater with gold rimmed glasses and a blue flower brooch pinned to her shoulder. When she looked up from her book, she nearly jumped off the stool with excitement. She practically threw down the book she was reading. As she weaved through the various items behind the counter, I glanced at the strange book she'd been reading. It was a deep blue with various silver markings I didn't recognize. But before I could inspect it closer, her petite, bony frame practically skipped over to me.

"Oh, I knew I'd get at least one more customer today. Welcome to Thistle Treasures. Can I help you find something special?"

"Uh, no, I'm just looking around."

"I think you are looking for something in particular." Her blue eyes sparkled with delight.

I shook my head. "I'm honestly not sure what I'm doing here, the place just drew me in."

The woman looked unphased. "That's a normal reaction. The place tends to have that effect on people. My name is Lavinia Thistle, but you can call me Vivi. This shop has been in my family for many generations." I began to look around in awe at the sheer volume of items that took up such a small space. A few vintage books on a shelf caught my eye.

"I can tell you so many stories about this place." Her eyes lit up as she was reliving those good memories.

I walked over to the stack of furniture, and found an old rocking chair in the corner. I reached out to touch the peeling paint.

"Oh I'd be careful with touching that one. It's a bit rickety."

I nodded and turned to scan the glass case at the counter. The case was filled with all sorts of jewelry. Necklaces, rings, bracelets, even a diamond tiara sat among the treasures. I was about to turn back to say goodbye, but something caught the corner of my eye. I turned back and saw a pair of earrings among the jewels shaped like dragonflies. They clearly weren't anything special. The metal was tarnished, but the wings held multi-colored stones that shimmered in the display case. At that moment, I knew I wanted them.

"How much for the earrings?" I asked the lady.

She frowned. "Which earrings might you be referring to?"

I blushed slightly. "The ones shaped like dragonflies. How much are they worth?"

A strange look came into her eye as she frowned at me. "How much they are worth is solely dependent on you." Nevertheless, she gave me a price that was surprisingly low. If I were in the city, I would've expected to pay triple for the pieces. My knowledge in art history didn't cover much about jewelry, but based on the craftsmanship, it suggested that they were from another decade.

"Do you know how old they are?" I asked as she rang up my order.
The woman shrugged. "Hard to say exactly. But I would say they are at least a hundred years old just looking at them. You should know that many of the items inside this building have existed for centuries. Like my parents, I try to preserve them, and give each object a second chance. Much like the one you are giving these fine specimens." She was about to put them in a box, but I wanted to try them on. She obliged and handed me a mirror.

It took a great amount of difficulty to put the earrings on. I'd avoided earrings altogether for a while after one of Byron's friends had said I had the wrong face shape for earrings. That comment confused me as much as it stung. But looking back, it stung even more because Byron never bothered to stand up for me. He'd just continued on like nothing had happened. Since then, I'd avoided wearing anything that drew attention to my face. But putting on the dragonfly earrings felt like a victory for me. A triumph. It felt like a much needed change. At that point, I didn't care how they made my face look, I just wanted to wear them with confidence.

I turned back to the counter. "Thank you ma'am. These are beautiful."

A smile spread across her face. "You are quite welcome dear. They look lovely. And please, call me Vivi, or Ms Thistle if you must. But I much prefer my friends to call me Vivi."

Vivi's smile was infectious, and I couldn't help myself. "I'm Ivy Zephyr. It was good to meet you Vivi."

As I left the small shop, I couldn't help but feel the need to visit again. Vivi Thistle seemed like a peculiar woman, and I wanted to learn more about her shop. Just as I made my way down the final step, I felt a strange tingle in my ears, but I brushed it off as just coming from the wind.

Chapter 5

The following day, I woke up early to go to work. Even though it would be a long day on my feet, I was excited. I showered and dressed in slacks and a pale blue shirt. I pulled my chestnut hair into a no nonsense low ponytail. Just as I was about to leave, I saw the dragonfly earrings winking up at me from my dresser. I considered leaving them, but decided I wanted to keep them close. I glanced in the mirror. The oval stones in the wings reflected a blue that matched my blue shirt perfectly, which made it official. I hurried down the stairs to the diner to help with the breakfast rush.

As I walked in, Lily greeted me at the counter. I tied an apron around my waist as she poured me a cup of coffee as I sat down for some food. After a few minutes, Mabel burst in with two stacks of pancakes. Only they weren't covered in the berry syrup I'd enjoyed yesterday.

"Blueberry pancakes are our daily special today." Mabel announced loudly even though there were no customers in the diner. "We ran out of strawberries yesterday, so we'll have to eighty-six the berry syrup until our next shipment."

I was disappointed at the loss of the triple berry syrup, but that changed as soon as I took a bite of the pancakes. I was never a huge fan of mushy blueberries in my pancakes growing up. But these pancakes not only had fresh blueberries that popped in my mouth, but there was a hint of lemon too. The pancakes were almost sour with the amount of lemon juice in the pancakes, but that was easily remedied with a dash of maple syrup. It was official, I was in a food paradise.

Lily noticed my smile. "Pretty good huh. I dare anyone to come in and tell Mabel that they don't like a certain food. I swear Mabel has the ability to make anyone like any food."

"You speak from experience?" I asked.

She smiled fondly. "My daughter refused to touch tomatoes for the longest time. But Mabel made her a hot panini with chicken, pesto, and cherry tomatoes. As soon as Olive took a bite, she couldn't stop. I've never had a problem with her and tomatoes since. Now if only I could do the same with mushrooms for myself."

Mabel laughed. "I'm afraid my cooking only goes so far, honey. I can often trick kids into liking a new food, but for adults, it's a lot harder. You already have a distaste for mushrooms, so to change your mind would be to change your entire outlook on the food itself."

Lily shrugged and turned to me. "I guess we can't like everything now can we?"

I nodded and smiled in agreement.

As soon as Lily turned the Closed sign to Open, we had customers. The sun was barely up, yet I'd seen a group of hungry teenagers drooling from hunger outside of the window for at least ten minutes before we opened.

I finished serving pancakes to two young girls when I heard the bell ring over the door. Out of the corner of my eye, I saw Amy on coffee duty, and Lily behind the counter. "Be right there." I called out to the customer behind me.

"Not a problem, I know what I want." I heard a familiar voice and turned around abruptly. Nolan was standing in the doorway with that same smirk on his face when we met on the street yesterday. For some reason he was wearing a leather jacket even though it was a hot late-summer day.

"I-"

"Can I get a cup of coffee here, or are my looks too much of a distraction?" I stared blankly, and didn't know how to answer, so he continued.

"If my looks are too much of an issue, I can fix that." He pulled a pair of aviator sunglasses from his pocket and put them on as if he was a cop in a movie, his face stoic and unmoving. He was clearly trying to look rugged and sharp as he folded his arms in front of his chest, but the sunglasses only made him look even more like a dork.

I couldn't help it, and burst out laughing.

Nolan whipped off the sunglasses and glared. "What's so funny?" That only made me laugh harder. If anyone else had done it, they would have succeeded. But Nolan's attempt at looking cool was anything but successful.

I was doubled over from laughing so hard, but I forced myself to stop and take a breath. "Nothing sorry, that just kind of caught me off guard." I sobered and felt my face burn when I saw his crestfallen face. "The sunglasses are cool," I blurted.

His eyes softened just slightly, and thankfully he put the sunglasses away as he sat down. I grabbed the coffee pot from Amy and poured him a cup. He took a long sip from the hot brew. Did everything have to be so dramatic with this guy? He was still trying to appear cool, but he was still failing miserably. I wanted nothing more than to tell him to drop the act already.

Nolan set down the cup and turned to me, I pulled out my notepad.

"What can I help you with today?" I asked in my best waitress voice.

The dork leaned in slowly and spoke softly, "A date might be nice."

Without thought, I gripped my pad so hard it folded. My knuckles were white, and I felt anger flood throughout my whole body.

Nolan nearly jumped back and his hands immediately up, "Woah, woah, easy. I was just kidding. I didn't think that would make you angry." His eyes were filled with fear, and I felt my face burn for the second time today. He was trying to be nice in a dorky sort of way, and I was being the jerk here. I put my notepad and pencil in my apron pocket and took a breath. I sat down in the chair opposite to him.

"I'm sorry. I don't know what came over me." That was a lie. I knew exactly what I was feeling. I wasn't mad at this guy, I was mad at the other guy in my life who was miles away at home and probably tanning by the side of his olympic sized pool without a care in the world.

"I've just had a strange past few days." I mumbled lamely.

He nodded. "Care to talk about it?"

I didn't want to talk about it anymore, but after my reaction, I felt I at least owed him an explanation.

"Remember how I told you I moved from San Francisco yesterday?"

Nolan smirked. "Yeah, but you didn't say why. I hate to break it to you, but statistically there's really not much out here to do compared to The Golden City. You need a really good reason to be out here."

"I caught my fiance cheating on me."

"That would do it." Realization dawned in Nolan's eyes, and he had the decency to look embarrassed. "I'm so sorry, I had no idea. I wouldn't have asked you if I'd known, I just-"

I put my hand up. "There is no way you would've known that. I'm sorry, you seem like a nice guy, I'm just in a rough place right now."

His eyes lit up. "Maybe what you need is a tour of the town. And I just so happen to be an expert in all things related to Redwood Bluff."

I felt my heart sink. "I'm not quite ready to date again. I was with my ex for over a year up until yesterday. I'm not the kind of girl just to hop right back into dating after a breakup."

Nolan shrugged. "That's fine. Because I technically didn't ask you out. I just simply asked if as a friend, you wanted a tour of the town. It would be short, and I promise not to ask you any personal questions. The only thing we will be discussing is the history of this fine rural piece of heaven." He leaned back in his chair with a newfound sense of dorky confidence.

I wanted to say no, but I did want to know more about this little town. I loved all things history, and the idea of having a friend was kind of nice. Maybe this would be a good first step in healing.

I took a page out of his book and paused dramatically while tapping my chin as if in thought. I had to admit, it was kind of fun to watch him squirm for a minute. I finally sat up and leaned in. "Ok, but only if we do this as friends. I do want to learn more about the town, but I don't want another relationship right now. Is that clear?"

The grin on his face was infectiously stupid, and I couldn't help but smile back. We exchanged numbers and agreed to meet up an hour after I finished work.

Chapter 6

As soon as Mabel's was closed, I ran up to my apartment to shower. Even though it was pleasantly warm outside, I'd helped Tom in the kitchen for a few hours that afternoon flipping burgers, and decided a shower was the best course of action before going out. I dug through my clothes and found a soft pink shirt and a fresh pair of black pants. Sandals and the dragonfly earrings helped to complete the look. I dried my hair and added a touch of mascara. Normally I would do a lot more to get ready, but I didn't want to give Nolan the wrong idea.

Nolan was waiting outside the diner in the same gray shirt he'd worn earlier. Thankfully he'd ditched the jacket and the sunglasses. I was glad he hadn't dressed up any more than I had.

As we walked down the mainstreet, Nolan pointed out the grocery store, the bookstore, the floral shop, and the local pharmacy. I had to admit, for a small town, it did well for itself. In addition to the diner, there were several other restaurants in Redwood Bluff. There were a couple of fast food joints, an ice cream parlor, and several bakeries. But Nolan said that the best spot for dinner was the Italian restaurant just down the street called Bistro Roma and we should eat. At that moment, I felt underdressed.

"I thought we agreed this was a casual get together with friends."

Nolan "Of course it is. For the record, I take all of my first dates to the funeral parlor."

My face paled and he laughed. "I'm totally kidding. Nah, I usually suggest a hike along the river trails. It's free, which makes me feel less guilty for ditching them in the woods afterwards."

I prayed he was joking. "I am game. Let's go. So how come you're taking me out to eat?"

He shrugged. "I figured it's your first time here, so you might as well try the Bistro at least once while you're in town."

When we were seated, our server with side swept hair and a faint Italian accent introduced himself as Alessandro. Even though I barely glanced at the menu, I knew exactly what I wanted the moment I saw it. Nolan ordered Penne al Pesto in a poor attempt at an Italian accent, while I ordered Fettuccine Alfredo. At that moment, my stomach needed something familiar. Alessandro simply rolled his eyes at Nolan, but managed a small smile as he took my order. I had no doubt this wasn't the first time he'd pretended to have an Italian accent.

While we ate, Nolan described his work as an architect. But I only half listened as I thought about mom. I wanted to talk to her, but I knew she still blamed me for leaving Byron.

Nolan noticed my silence. "Are you thinking about your ex?" he whispered.

I shook my head and sipped my glass of water. "No, I had a fight with my mom shortly after I caught him cheating."

"What was it about?"

I shrugged. "She wanted me to stay with him just because he's rich, and he can take care of me."

"And you disagree?"

I hesitated. I wasn't sure how much I wanted to tell this man I'd only met yesterday. "My dad left me when I was young. My mom thinks it's better to marry rich because you never know when he's going to cheat."

Nolan put down his fork. "Do you agree with her?" Nolan's eyes were serious.

I stared at my plate. "I don't know. I didn't want to agree with her, but within the past few days, I've started to reconsider. It hurts because I told her that he was different. I wanted him to be different, but after what he did, I'm starting to see how she felt when my dad left."

I continued to stare at my plate as I fought back tears. This was not how I wanted the date to go.I desperately tried to think of something else to talk about, but Nolan interrupted my thoughts.

"Um. Ivy. Your earrings are glowing?"

I thought he was joking at first, so I pulled off an earring to prove they weren't, but I was wrong. The earring was glowing a soft blue. I put my hand over it in case it was just reflected light, but it wasn't. The earring was glowing almost as bright as the flashlight on my phone. The phenomenon was strange.

At that moment, the earring stopped glowing. Shocked that it turned off as I stared a little longer. I slipped the earring back into my ear and took one more sip of my water.

"I think I should get back. I have an early morning tomorrow."

Nolan looked disappointed, and I felt bad. But I was exhausted, and the events of the past few days were starting to hit me.

As we walked back to the diner talking about the town, I saw Thistle Treasures on the corner. At that moment, I wanted to return the earrings. The last thing I needed was a pair of freaky glowing earrings in my life. I'd return them and say that I needed my money back. That wasn't true, but I didn't know how to explain that the earrings had made me feel very uneasy. Almost as if something was about to happen.

Chapter 7

The next morning at the diner was the same as before. The only thing that changed was Mabel switching out blueberry pancakes for french toast as the daily special.

I decided to take the earring back to the antique shop on my lunch break. I wanted them gone as soon as possible. But as soon as I arrived at Thistle Treasures, I nearly forgot about returning the earrings.

As soon as I turned the corner, I saw the streets in front of the shop lined with police cars. Without thinking, I ran inside the shop to see Vivi being interrogated by a blonde female and two male officers, one blonde and the other with jet black hair. All three wore badges and holstered guns on their belts.

"Hey, what's going on?" I walked over to the counter where Vivi sat almost comfortably but not quite.

The female officer motioned for the blonde haired officer, definitely the younger of the two, to show me out. Based on how they responded to her, she was clearly the one in charge.

"What is your business?" The officer was clearly trying to push me out.

"What's going on?" I retorted.

"There's been an incident. We're just making our rounds. There's nothing more to see here."

I was about to leave, when Vivi stood up and walked over to me.

"Ivy, there you are. I'm so glad you made it." Vivi pulled me in for a hug, I leaned in and she spoke softly into my ear.

"These officers are accusing me of murder. I need a friend. Help me please."

I was about to refuse as I pulled out of the hug, but behind the hair and the gold rimmed glasses, I saw Vivi's pale eyes were filled with fear. Real fear. I couldn't help it. I took pity on the old woman and caved.

I walked over to the female officer. "What is going on here?"

Her blue eyes narrowed. "And who are you?"

I straightened my shoulders. I wasn't ready to step down from a challenge. "Ivy Zephyr, and I won't ask again. You mentioned an incident?"

The officer paused, clearly trying to decide how much information to give out. Her face finally relaxed, and I hoped it meant she would talk.

"What is your relationship with this woman?" Her voice was almost kind, but she still meant all business. I was about to say I didn't know, but Vivi stepped in.

"She's my granddaughter Chief Lawson. Now please explain to her why you are accusing me of killing Mr. Bellman." Vivi responded with confidence. I tried to keep my face neutral, but her lying to the police officer completely caught me off guard.

The blonde woman, Chief Lawson apparently, walked toward me.

"Very well Mrs. Zephyr."

"It's Ms. actually-" I corrected.

"My apologies." She smiled again, and this time it seemed almost genuine. But her icy blue eyes still set me on edge.

"I am Chief Lawson. My deputies and I are investigating the death of Mr. Bellman. At first we thought it was an accident, but there were some things that appeared… suspicious."

"How suspicious?" I asked. Wasn't all death supposed to be suspicious?

"He was stabbed in the back with a letter opener." Made sense to me.

"But what does that have to do with me?" Vivi asked.

Chief Lawson nodded to the officers behind her. The dark haired officer pulled out a photograph and handed it to the chief. He stood a full foot above her, but even so, she was still clearly in charge.

The photograph showed a tarnished, silver antique letter opener covered in blood. The chief explained that the letter opener had been traced back to Thistle Treasures.

"How?" I asked.

"There was a receipt for the letter opener in the wastebasket in Mr. Bellman's office."

"But can you prove that it came from this store?" I was on the defense.

Vivi piped up. "I did sell Mr. Bellman that letter opener. An old silver letter opener made in Spain toward the beginning of the 20th century."

I was confused. "Just because she sold him the letter opener doesn't mean that she stabbed him with it. If anything, it should clear her of suspicion because it was bought fair and square." I felt more confident with each word.

Chief Lawson's face turned grim. "True, but we also found several antique items in his office with tags from this store."

"Like what?" I was starting to feel impatient.

"An old lamp, a flower vase, book ends, and a small statue of a lion."

"But what does that have to do with me chief? Yes, I sold him all of those, but Mr. Bellman was one of my best buyers. He's quite the collector of antiques. Especially his coin collection. I've been on the lookout for coins to sell him, but nothing's come up lately."

"Has Mr. Bellman ever stolen from you before?" The dark haired officer finally spoke with a deep rich baritone voice as I turned to the officer. I couldn't help it. My heart fluttered just slightly.

Vivi shook her head. "No, he was an honest man." I sighed with relief. "But," I felt my heart tense as Vivi spoke that dreaded word. "His time was almost near. I didn't expect him to depart last night, but I can't say I'm surprised."

"So you admit to killing him?" All three officers looked a little too eager for my liking. I was sure I saw the blonde male officer reaching for his handcuffs.

"I didn't say that, I only said he was close to death and complained about getting much sicker lately. From the way it looks, someone simply helped him to finish the transition to the next life." She shrugged with a strange look on her face.

I wanted to scream. Vivi had basically confessed to killing him. What had I gotten myself into? Oh right. I was trying to return a pair of creepy earrings to a potential psychopath disguised as a sweet old lady. Why didn't I just throw the earrings in the trash? Or burn them? At that moment, the earrings felt heavy in my pocket.

Chief Lawson looked almost smug as she reached for her handcuffs. I couldn't decide which side I was on. But the dark haired officer grabbed his superior by the arm before she could make another move.

"Chief, with all due respect, we need solid evidence."

"Stand down Detective Merrick." My eyes lit up as I finally put a name to the officer.

"But ma'am-"

"She just confessed. I need this case wrapped up as soon as possible. I've got the city down my neck enough already. The last thing this department needs is another drawn out case."

The blonde man walked to stand between us and Chief Lawson. "Merrick's right. We can't just arrest her because it's convenient. You may have a hunch, but that doesn't mean she's guilty."

"Exactly. Thank you Marshall." Merrick turned back to the chief. "We can't arrest her right now. It'll be less messy to take our time and get it right later."

Her blue eyes blazed, but Merrick put his hand up as if this was a common thing. "The last thing we need is bad publicity, I agree. But don't you think this will be even worse publicity for us if we arrest the wrong person right away."

With that, Detective Merrick motioned the Chief out of the antique shop, and Marshall followed behind. He handed Vivi a card and warned us both that we'd hear back from them soon. As soon as the door was closed, I breathed a sigh of relief.

Chapter 8

After the officers left, I turned to Vivi, who had conveniently disappeared. I called for her.

"In the kitchen dear. No need to shout." The old woman scolded as she returned with a glass of milk and a plate of cookies. She walked as if without a care in the world. I was sure she would've been skipping with joy if she wasn't carrying a tray. I couldn't help it, this woman was crazy, but she made me laugh. I noticed that she was wearing another brooch pinned to her jacket. Today, she wore a gold brooch shaped like a marigold. Very fitting considering that someone was dead. I wondered if it was really a coincidence, or if this sweet little old lady was really a murderer.

Vivi offered me the plate of chocolate chip cookies, but I refused. I didn't want to take any chances.

Vivi looked surprisingly calm. "I don't blame you for being cautious dear. I apologize for roping you in, but those officers were getting on my nerves. I don't appreciate people who come in and accuse me of using priceless pieces of art to murder my patrons."

"Patrons?" I asked.

"Mr. Bellman was one of my best buyers. He had an eye for valuable pieces. There is no way I would have wanted him dead."

"I still don't understand why I'm a part of this." I told her.

Vivi's face still was strangely calm. "Those officers were ready to arrest me and close the case. I didn't mean to pull you into my problem, but I hoped that you would help them to see that their evidence was circumstantial at best. Fortunately, you helped to do so, so thank you for that."

I nodded. I had to admit, I probably would have done the same if I was in her shoes.

"So what do we do now?" I asked.

"We?" Vivi looked hopeful.

I nodded. This woman was crazy, but there was something about her that intrigued me. I was curious to find out if she was really the killer or not. The thought of playing detective felt exciting. If anything, this would be a good way to take my mind off my own problems.

"Do you think this is a frame job?" I asked.

"Frame job?"

I flushed slightly. "You know? Someone else wants to set up the murder so you will be arrested?" Vivi's eyes nodded in recognition. "You think someone wanted me to get arrested."

I nodded. "Can you think of anyone who might be angry at you?"

Vivi shook her head. "I don't know. I don't get a lot of customers these days. I've been warned by the bank that if I don't improve sales, I might lose the place." She looked sad at the thought, and I decided to change the subject.

"How long have you worked here?" I asked.

Vivi's eyes lit up immediately. "For as long as I can remember. My grandparents built this shop when they immigrated from Europe many years ago. Ma and Pa helped in the shop my whole life, and I started helping after school. When my parents passed, the place became mine. I've been trying to run it just as they did, but business has slowed down for the last couple of years. Just seems like bad luck and people don't like to visit anymore. Maybe it has come time to shut it down."

"Do you think anyone at the bank might be eager for you to sell?"

Vivi paused for a moment. "Now that you mention it, there's this crabby little accountant who's been encouraging me to sell for months now. He keeps promising me a decent payout. That wouldn't be as bad if he didn't keep telling me to move into a retirement home every time I visit."

"Who is the accountant?" I asked her.

"His name is Billy Archend."

I nodded. I was still new to the town, so I didn't know where to find the bank, or anything about a Billy Archend.

Then it hit me. Nolan had offered to give me more tours of the town. Maybe he would know something about Archend that could help take the heat off Vivi for a while.

Chapter 9

"Hello?"

Nolan's voice was eager, and I almost regretted asking for his help.

"Hey Nolan, I need your help."

"Your wish is my command, m'lady." I rolled my eyes. He was honestly too much sometimes.

"I don't know if you've heard, but there's been a murder-"

"Oh, you mean the murder that's on the news right now. Yeah, I heard. Didn't know the guy, but still sad you know."

News really did travel fast in a small town. "The police think Vivi did it. I don't think she's guilty."

"The lady at the antique store on the corner? What were you doing there?"

For some reason it felt strange that Nolan knew Vivi. I wondered if it was just a small town thing. "Yeah that's the one. That's where I bought the earrings I wore last night. I was trying to return them today, but the police were there and-"

"Return them? Why? That glow trick was so cool."
He was clearly in awe.

"If you want to wear them, be my guest, but I want
nothing to do with them."

"I would wear them, but they would make my ears
look too big in proportion to my head." I almost
laughed. "Besides, they looked nice on you last
night."

I felt my cheeks turn pink. "Thank you, that's very
sweet of you. But the police said the murder
happened last night. I don't think it was a
coincidence that the earrings glowed last night too.
Either way, they feel like a bad omen. Last thing I
need is more bad luck in my life."

"Then why are you investigating the murder?"

I sat up. "I didn't say I was investigating."

"You didn't have to. You clearly want to figure out
what happened. Don't you?"

I sighed in defeat. So much for being subtle.
"Yes?..."

"And you need my help to solve it because I am so
very experienced in our beloved town and you are
very-" he was clearly trying to be delicate.

"-inexperienced." I decided to save him the trouble.

"I was going to say you're unfamiliar with the town layout, but that works too."

I rolled my eyes again. "Anyway, I think I might have a lead. I want to clear Vivi, but I need help. Are you in?"

"Why are you helping her?" Nolan's voice had a slight edge that caught me off guard.

"Why shouldn't I? She could use help. Do you have something against her?"

"Something's off about her. Everyone in town knows it. She's always constantly mumbling to herself, and she's got an uncanny ability in predicting the future. Specifically predicting when someone is about to die. There were always stories about her family but they mostly kept to themselves."

That made the hair on the back of my neck stand up. "Predicting when someone is about to die? How often does she do that?"

"Not very often. But I had an old work buddy a few years back. Emphasis on old. More like ancient. The guy was at least a hundred or something. Anyway, he walked into the shop one day, and was dead the next."

I rolled my eyes. "That feels more like a coincidence than a prediction. You said so yourself, the guy was probably on death's doorstep."

Nolan gave a low growl that felt out of character. "That's not the weirdest one. There was another incident several years back. A young boy walked out of the antique shop with a couple of buddies. An hour later, there was a car crash. The only reason they made a link to her was because one of the boys survived to tell the tale. Everyone in town has some weird story about her. I guess some are good but lately they seem to hold bad omens."

"I still don't get it. You're all mad just because she can predict death?"

Nolan's voice showed he was annoyed. "No, people wonder whether she's the cause of the deaths or if she just knows things. I'm all for protecting the innocent, but I still don't trust her. We've had a weird few years in a row with people getting sick and weather being nastier than normal."

I saw an opening. "I think Vivi might be innocent. I want to prove it. That or prove that she's guilty. Either way, I want to help solve the case."

"Are you a detective now?"

I paused for a moment. "No, but it's a good distraction from my problems to solve this one."

That seemed to satisfy Nolan. I told him about Billy Archend at the bank, and he agreed it was a good lead. We agreed to meet at the bank later, right when the bank was closing.

Chapter 10

The bank was a bust.

We arrived at the bank right at closing. I was worried we'd miss the bank completely, but we caught a bank teller in red heels wearing a delicate gold chain. We managed to stop her just as she was locking the door and preparing to leave. She introduced herself as Lydia Morgan. We asked her about Billy Archend, but she said he'd been out of town for the past two weeks on business.

"Did he ever mention what type of business?" I asked the young girl.

She shook her head rapidly. Her cropped brunette hair brushed across her shoulders as she moved. "No one knows for sure. But there's a rumor going around in the office that he's in Vegas living it up." The thought made me feel uncomfortable. I didn't even know the man and I already disliked him even more.

Nolan finally spoke up. "Does Mr. Archend have any issues with Thistle Treasures."

Lydia's eyes lit up in recognition. "He's been trying to get the owner to sell for a long time. But I think he's finally close to giving up. He keeps talking about leaving to start a new business venture in the city. But then again, it's not the first time he's tried a fast get rich scheme."

I decided to try a different approach. "Do you know Mr. Bellman?"

Lydia's eyes began to fill with tears. "Yes, I heard about his death." Her words were short and precise despite the tears.

"You knew him personally?" Nolan asked.

Lydia nodded. "His son was my ex-fiancee. We broke it off just a few months before the wedding." Her voice cracked halfway through the last word.

My heart panged as I remembered my own wedding. I wondered if Byron had finished canceling the catering and the florists yet. Knowing him, he probably hadn't even bothered to start.

"What happened?" I asked.

The young girl shrugged. "He was cheating on me. I called him out for it, but he denied it. I didn't want to take the chance that he'd cheat again after we got married. I called it off the next day."

Nolan nodded. "How did Mr. Bellman take the news?"

The tears in Lydia's eyes began to fall. She tried to hide it, but finally gave up. "He never approved of the marriage. We didn't send him an invite to the wedding. He kept saying that I would never be good enough for his perfect son. He said that I would never join his family until the day he died."

This was good. Maybe we were finally making progress. "Did they ever say how he died?"

She nodded. "They said he died suddenly so I assumed it was a heart attack. Which seemed odd because he didn't have a heart condition. Considering his age, he was in remarkably good health. A week ago, I would've been glad he was gone, but now I just feel guilty for thinking such a horrible thing." As she spoke, Lydia dug in her red purse. She pulled out a folder filled with papers, a pack of mints, a gold hand mirror, and several tubes of lipstick. Finally, she pulled out a lanyard with car keys on the end. Hot tears fell from her face and she tried to brush them away. I wanted to hug her, but feared it wasn't the right time.

"Why is that?" Nolan's face was steely, yet his eyes full of concern.

"A week ago, I would've done anything to be with my ex. But now, I want nothing to do with either of them."

I needed to change the subject before I started crying. "Can you think of anyone that might want Mr. Bellman dead?"

Lydia paused for a moment. "Come to think of it, there's this one gallery owner who's been trying to sell his artwork to the big boys. Mr. Bellman tried to ignore him, but the man was persistent. He warned him that he would regret not buying his artwork right away. The crazy man really believes that he's going to become a famous artist, but I can't think of anyone who would want a creepy painting of skulls to celebrate death like that.

I felt the back of my neck prickle as I remembered the man who'd tried to sell me a creepy painting just like that the day before. "This man doesn't by chance go by the name Gregor?"

Lydia nodded. "That's the one."

"The gallery goblin? That guy's weird." Nolan agreed.

"Gallery goblin?" I furrowed my brows, but both Nolan and Lydia nodded in recognition.

"It's just the town that calls him that. Most people believe he's the main problem we're struggling to get tourists." Lydia explained.

I nodded slowly. "Do you think he'd be capable of murder?"

Lydia shrugged. "Hard to say. Mr. Bellman was a complicated man. Most people believe that he loved his antiques more than his own son. I wouldn't be surprised if he made the man angry enough to kill."

Nolan and I didn't say a word until we got into his truck.

"She's hiding something." Nolan was the first to speak.

I nodded. I'd been thinking the same thing. Lydia had every motivation to kill her soon to be father in law. But the timing didn't feel quite right. It was possible she could've been lying about wanting to break up with her ex to cover her tracks.

"Do you think she's telling the truth?" I finally asked Nolan as he drove away from the bank.

He shrugged as he turned toward the diner. "Hard to say. They'd already planned to get married in secret. It's possible they still are planning to get married in secret."

"But why?"

"Don't you get it. If they planned to murder Mr. Bellman together, they would've been the easiest suspects. The police always suspect the family first. But if they were broken up already, a murder would be a perfect excuse for them to get back together. Bond over their grief. It's almost perfect."

I nodded. It seemed like a good plan. But we needed proof. We needed a second witness.

"I think we need to pay a visit to Mr. Bellman's son." I felt almost giddy as I said the words.

Nolan nodded as he pulled up to the diner. "I'll make some phone calls tonight. I'll let you know if I find out anything about him. Meanwhile, keep your door locked tonight."

"Why?" I asked.

"There's a murderer afoot, and we must be prepared Watson."

I frowned. "Wait a minute, I started this investigation. That makes me Sherlock." I opened the door.

Nolan rolled down the window. "But I do a better accent. Therefore, I be the better Watson, lassie." He gave me that same boyish smile.

I rolled my eyes. "That was more Scottish than British young lad. Best keep up if you wish to play with the big boys." I ran for the diner before he had a chance to respond. However, I was met with a large honk as I ran in front of the truck. I nearly jumped as Nolan drove away. He was clearly laughing, and my face burned.

Chapter 11

The next day went by without a word from Nolan. I tried not to think about the investigation, but that was harder than I thought.

As I served chocolate chip pancakes to an elderly couple, I heard the doorbell ring. I hoped it was Nolan with news about Gregor or Billy Archend, but I was instead greeted by a young man with a square jaw and a scowl on his face.

I took a deep breath and plastered a smile on my face. "Hi, welcome to Mabel's diner. Can I help you with anything?"

"Yeah, you can take my order. I've been waiting forever." Every part of me wanted to point out that he'd just walked into the place less than five minutes ago. I was just about to bring him a menu, but he'd approached me before I had a chance to do so.

"Of course sir. I'll get you a menu right away."
His eyes were still hard and clearly annoyed as he took a seat. I snatched a menu from the counter. Last thing I needed today was an angry customer in my already bad mood. I sighed with relief when he opened the menu without complaint. That could have escalated so fast.

The man ordered eggs and hashbrowns. Just as I was pouring him a cup of coffee, the bell above the door jingled, and in stepped the dark haired Detective Merricks. I felt my heart flutter just slightly as I saw his face, but quickly pushed it down.

"Where's your boss?" I called to him as he neared me.

"At the station. I came to talk to him." He gave me a little smile as he pointed at my customer who sipped his coffee while glaring at Merrick. His posture was still and businesslike. I felt as if I'd just walked into an arena with two angry lions about to fight.

"Can I get you anything?" I asked the officer.

"Just coffee. I'm not staying long." Merrick turned to the table. "Can we talk, Mr. Bellman?" Neither man responded for a long time. They just stared at each other as if daring the other to make the first move. I felt my heart pounding, and I feared things were going to get ugly, so I tried to deescalate the situation.

"Bellman." I blurted out. "You mean like Mr. Bellman from the news?" I regretted the words as soon as they slipped out. Why couldn't I just ask about the weather like a normal person?

That caused both men to break the tension. The young Mr. Bellman set down his cup and nodded grimly. "Richard Bellman was my father." He turned to Officer Merrick. "Call me Jonah."

The officer sat down and began to talk to Jonah. "Mr. Bellman, first of all, on behalf of the Police-"

"-what do you want? I know you're not here just to pay respect to my old man." Jonah's face turned from bothered to completely annoyed. Something about him made me mad, but I couldn't place it.

Detective Merrick clearly was trying a different approach. "Mr Bellman-"

"Jonah. My name is Jonah." Jonah was getting more annoying by the second.

"Very well, Jonah." The dark haired officer pulled out a notepad from his pocket. "Where were you the night your father was murdered?"

Now that was a juicy detail. I began to refill all of the coffee cups within the vicinity of the table. I refilled several cups even before the customers had a chance to take a sip."
Despite my attempts, the boys spoke in such low voices, I couldn't make out anything other than their facial expressions. I watched Jonah drain the last of his cup, and saw my chance. They made no

attempt to stop talking as I refilled both cups as slowly as I could.

"-and that is why I need to find my fathers killer. I need this settled as soon as possible."

Officer Merrick scribbled in his notebook. I tried to casually peer down at his scrawled words, but they were a complete jumbled mess. What was it with police officers and scribbled handwriting? Didn't they have to submit police reports or something? Merrick's voice snapped me out of my thoughts.

"I assure you Jonah, we are doing everything we can. The police want this case wrapped up just as fast as you."

Jonah nodded and called for the check. Once his meal was paid for, he left without another word. I was about to leave when the still sitting officer held up his mug for a refill. How many cups of coffee could this guy drink?

I poured him a cup and he took another long sip. I groaned mentally. Did all the men in this town sip their coffee dramatically for sport? He was even worse than Nolan. But at least he wasn't wearing aviator sunglasses.

After draining his cup, the detective finally looked at me. He motioned for me to sit down across from him. I decided to hear him out as I set the coffee pot on the table between us.

Detective Merricks leaned in. "I'm aware that you've been doing a bit of investigating around town."

"Excuse me?" I felt fear inside of me, but decided to deny it.

"I've gotten word about you traveling around town. First the antique shop, then the bank. Also, you really need to learn how to spy on people better as a waitress." That last comment was uncalled for. "My point is, you're sticking your nose where it doesn't belong."

"Why would I do that? I have a job, you know. I don't just run around sticking my nose into things that I don't care about." That wasn't completely a lie. Even if I wasn't completely sure how I felt about Vivi, a part of me still believed she could be innocent.

"The police department has been under enough scrutiny already. The last thing we need is for a civilian to step in and get hurt while attempting to do our job. Is that clear?"

Now I was annoyed. "For the record, I'm not attempting to do your job. I am doing your job. Did you know about the link between the bank and Vivi? Apparently a Mr. Archend-"

"-has been pushing Miss Thistle to sell for a long time. That's not new to this town. A lot of people want her to sell the place." said Officer Merrick.

"And what about Gregor the gallery artist? He has a connection to Mr. Bellman through-"

He continued, "His attempts to sell his artwork in exchange for publicity. We've had numerous restraining orders placed on him for harassing people to buy his stuff. Guy seems more desperate than anything. He's a creepy dude, but if anyone's guilty of murder, it's Ms. Thistle."

That appeared to be the consensus with Vivi. Everyone in the town seemed to hate her. "But why her?"

"She's bad news. We've tried to leave her alone, but there's gossip going around that anyone who sets foot in that place is doomed to die."

"I've been there. I'm not dead."

"Not yet." The officer's smile sent a chill down my back. But at that moment, I only felt angry.

"I don't care what rumors you believe. I've met Vivi, and yes she may be odd. But I don't think being a little different is equivalent to being a murderer. Have you even met her?"

"Yes, I saw her yesterday when I went to interview her." Merrick's emerald colored eyes seethed with annoyance.

I felt my face burn. How could I forget? Why didn't I keep my mouth shut? My anger boiled, and I feared I would lose it.

Despite my anger, I tried to remain cordial. "Right. Is there anything else you came to say?" I felt the sarcasm and the annoyance dripping from my voice, but even so I refused to back down.

However, it looked like this officer had a bit of a temper too. I felt like his green eyes were piercing through and staring straight at my soul with a ferocious intensity. "Please Miss Zephyr. I don't want you to get hurt," His voice was almost gentle. "I need you to be safe because-"

"Because?" I felt my heart speed up just momentarily. A lot could be said with just that word.

"-because that would be bad press for the police department, and we are already under enough pressure to succeed." His justification felt like a backhanded compliment.

"What kind of pressure? Everyone seems to keep bringing it up." I had to change tactics before I lost my head.

I didn't think it was possible, but the officer managed to put up a second wall. I could see it in his face. "We failed to save a life. We didn't follow up on a suspect, and he got away. He killed again, and of course, the media always blames the cops. No matter what we do, they only see the worst in us." He looked dejected with this statement. I almost felt sorry for him. Almost, but not quite.

"How does this affect your current case?" I kept my voice hard.

Merrick steeled his eyes. "It shouldn't. Yet it still does. Everyone is on eggshells because they're terrified of making another mistake. That's not the way to work." With a final swig, Merrick set down his cup and pulled out a few bills. He slapped them down on the counter and stormed out without a second glance.

Chapter 12

"Just like that? He left without another word?"
Nolan's voice on the phone was so eager, it felt like
sharing teenage girl gossip all over again.

"Yep. He just left without a word." I paused before I
asked the question weighing on my mind.
"Detective Merrick mentioned a previous case that
put extra pressure on the entire department. Do
you know anything about that?" I sucked in a breath
and crossed my fingers.

"How could I forget? It was all over the news.
Basically they were following the case of a
suspected serial killer who was passing through
Redwood Bluff. He or she killed several individuals,
but none had any connections."

My heart froze. The last thing I needed was to be in
the same town as a serial killer. "Do they know
anything about him or her?" I felt my chest pound,
but I had to know.

Nolan shifted on the other line. "The victims were
all of different ages, sexes, and occupations. The
pattern suggests that it might be a male."

"How so? Girls can be serial killers." I mentally
slapped myself and my overzealous feminism.

"Female serial killers are more likely to target vulnerable people or people they know. Male killers are more likely to target a stranger."

"How do you know they're strangers?" I asked.

"There's no connection between any of them as far as I can tell." Nolan's voice sounded disappointed. This was a puzzle, and he wanted to solve it as much as I did.

"We need to regroup and come up with a new plan."

"We? Did you not hear mister not so nice cop's warning? He told you to stay away. Imagine what he'll say when he finds out you went behind his back."

I knew Nolan was right. I had to be discreet. If I got caught, I didn't want to think what would happen. We needed a place where we wouldn't get caught. Somewhere the police wouldn't bother us as we worked the case. Then it hit me.

I put my phone back to my ear. "Are you free tonight?"

Nolan was clearly hesitant. "Yeah sure, but where can we go? The police are watching the entire town with an eagle eye." There was a pause on the line. "Wait, maybe we can meet up at my place. Or your place? Maybe we can order pizza and a movie or something too?"

I couldn't decide whether to feel happy or annoyed at that remark. "Actually, I was thinking we could meet at Thistle Treasures."

"You mean the place with the crazy old murder suspect lady? Are you sure that's a good idea? What if she's guilty?"

I wanted to scream, but took a deep breath. "You don't know that. Besides, the police are afraid of her too. They'll leave us alone once we're inside." I kept my voice low, almost as if I was calming a child.

Nolan's voice rose an octave. "Yeah, but that also means no chance of calling the police when she starts chasing us with a chainsaw." I almost burst out laughing, but suppressed it when I didn't hear laughing on the other end.

"Vivi with a chainsaw? I sincerely doubt it. If anything, she'll probably poison us. Just don't eat anything she offers."

Nolan gave a shaky sigh. "Fine, we'll do it. But if things go bad, it's on you."

"Fair enough." We agreed to meet up in a half hour. I really hoped that Nolan was wrong about Vivi, and

that we would be walking into a quaint shop and not
a serial killer's home.

Chapter 13

We got to Thistle Treasures by 6pm. Despite the store still being open for a little longer, the entire place was deserted. The streets surrounding the shop were empty too, as if everyone was avoiding the little antique store. I wondered if this was normal, or if last night's news had anything to do with it. As we walked toward the front desk, we saw Vivi with the same blue book in her hand. Her face lit up as she recognized me.

"Ivy. What a pleasant surprise. And who is your friend?" Vivi wore a silver butterfly brooch today with emerald gemstones in the wings. I mentally kicked myself for not bringing back the dragonfly earrings she'd given me. The further I got into this case, the less I wanted them.

"Vivi, this is Nolan. He's been showing me around town." Nolan's face seemed to get whiter with every passing second. For a moment, I was afraid he'd pass out. "Nolan, this is Vivi." I looped my arm through his in hopes of stabilizing him.

Vivi noticed the same thing I did. "I think you better sit down young man. You look like you've just seen a ghost." We helped Nolan to sit down on a small stool behind the counter.

"I'll make some tea for us. You both look as if you could use some." With that, Vivi slipped through a doorway to the kitchen.

I turned to Nolan. "Are you ok?" I asked.

Nolan's lips moved, but no words came out. I shook him gently, and finally sounds began to emerge from his mouth.

"She's the one. The one everyone talks about. She-she- she's going to murder us both."
I refrained from rolling my eyes. "Oh please, don't be so melodramatic."

He glared at me. "You were the one who said she'd poison us."

"You thought she was going to chase us with a chainsaw like a maniac. And I meant the poison thing as a joke. Come on, she's a sweet old lady. Now pull yourself together."

At that moment, Vivi returned with a tray of tea and a platter of cookies similar to the ones from my last visit to the store. I helped Nolan to a seat at a larger table, and sat down across from him, with both of us on either side of Vivi who sat at the head.

After an awkward moment of silence, Vivi finally broke the peace. "Alright. I get it. You younglings think I'm here to poison you. Or suffocate you.

Whichever you prefer. I assure you, if I were going to do it, I wouldn't do it here. Blood is impossible to remove from Oak."

I felt like smiling. I felt almost relieved. But Nolan still said nothing. "Actually it was a chainsaw".

She giggled at that one. Then we sat in more silence for a bit.

Vivi sighed dramatically. "Fine, if you're not going to eat or drink anything, then I will." With that, she poured herself a cup of tea, and helped herself to one of the cookies on the plate. That was enough for me and I followed suit. The cookies were perfectly sweet and crumbly.

Vivi handed out the plate to Nolan, who still refused to touch her cookies. I decided to change the subject.

"Vivi, we need your help." The old lady carefully set down the plate of cookies and turned to me with full attention.

"The police aren't happy that we've been investigating. We need a place to do our research in peace and-"

"-and you want to regroup here because the police won't dare set foot in here." Vivi's jaw was hard, yet her eyes were gentle.

I took a deep breath. "Yes. And maybe you can give us a new perspective on the case. We're fresh out of suspects at the moment."

Vivi took another sip of her tea. "Tell me everything."

At that point, Nolan decided to finally speak up. "At first we thought Mr. Archend from the bank could have a motive. But he was out of town when the murder was committed."

"What other suspects do you have?" Vivi took another bite of a cookie and held the plate to Nolan.

Nolan took the plate from her hands before setting it back down on the tray again without taking a cookie. "We thought about Gregor the gallery goblin-"

The old woman scoffed. "Oh please, Gregor has no backbone in his body. The day he does anything as insane as killing a person will be the day I die."

Those last words sent a shiver down my spine, and Nolan was clearly thinking the same thing.

"So if he's not guilty, then we're fresh out of suspects." Nolan squeaked.

Vivi nodded. "Very well, I'll help you. I want this case wrapped up just as much as you do. Maybe even more so. After all, I'm the one to blame if we don't figure out who murdered Mr. Bellman."

Chapter 14

We spent the next several hours at Thistle Treasures. Luckily, Vivi kept a thorough record of her customers' receipts, and we began to go through to find any clues. We had to start at the beginning and work our way out.

"I didn't realize that Mr. Bellman came in so often. I've found at least a dozen receipts with his name." I called out to the other two.

"Make that a dozen plus one. I've found another." Nolan handed me the scrap of paper.

I frowned. "Still a dozen mister. This isn't for a Richard Bellman, it's for a Jonah Bellman."

Vivi furrowed her eyebrows, and I rushed to explain.

"Jonah is Mr. Bellman's son. Do you know him? Dark hair and tall frame?"

Vivi paused for a moment. "Come to think of it, yes. A young man striking that resemblance came in last week."

I quickly stood up. "What did he buy?" Nolan leaned in to hear.

The woman simply shrugged. "Not much I'm afraid. He bought a small vintage handheld mirror. Pretty, but definitely had seen better days."

Nolan frowned. "What do you mean?"

"The brass handle was tarnished, and it needed a good cleaning. I offered to sell him a polished silver mirror instead, but he insisted on gold trim. Very odd young man."

A small gold mirror. Where had I seen a small gold mirror hand mirror?

Then it hit me. The young girl from the bank. What was her name? Lydia. She'd pulled out a strange looking mirror from her bag. I'd only seen it for a moment, but it had been gold, and it definitely wasn't new. Could it just be a coincidence? I had to know.

"I, I have to go." I quickly grabbed my bag and ran out before Nolan or Vivi could stop me. As I ran toward the bank, I felt my phone buzz. Probably Nolan. I decided to ignore it.

When I got to the bank, I realized that it was still early afternoon. Lydia was probably working right now. What was I going to do? Could I pose as a customer? Should I wait? I paced back and forth. But just then, Lydia walked out the bank in a tan suit and black flats. She carried the exact same red purse as the day before. Luck was on my side today.

I ran over to her. "Hey, Lydia right? Ivy. Remember we met yesterday?"

Lydia's pupils dilated. "Oh right. You and your boyfriend came in and began interrogating me about my love life." Her face was clearly annoyed, and I knew I had to tread carefully.

I put my hands up in defense. "First of all, I'm really sorry for that. But yesterday I saw a mirror in your bag. Do you by chance still have it?"

Her face shifted from annoyed to confused. She paused for a long time, clearly deciding whether or not to trust me. After several minutes, she reached into her bag and pulled out the mirror I'd seen yesterday. She handed it to me. The hand mirror felt heavy in my hand, and it was just as Vivi had described it: tarnished and clearly well loved in another era. I fingered the mirror, and found it had been cracked clean through in the top right corner. Aside from that, it was a beautiful piece.

"Where did you get this?" I asked her cautiously.

Lydia shrugged. "My ex-fiancee showed up a few days ago asking to get back together with me. He gave me the mirror in hopes of patching up our relationship."

"But why an antique mirror?" I'd heard of a guy giving a girl jewelry. But a hand mirror seemed a bit unusual.

She fingered the gold chain around her neck. "I honestly have no idea. Maybe it's because I wear a lot of gold? But I know his father collects a lot of antiques, so maybe he gave his son the idea."

"What did you do when he gave you the mirror?"

"I told him to get away from me. I called him a cheater and told him to never come near me again. I'm not proud of the other things I said, but I wanted nothing to do with him."

My eyes began to sting as I remembered my own problems with my ex. Even though I barely knew this woman, I could relate to what she was going through, and that only made my heart hurt for her.

"Was your ex Jonah Bellman?" I knew it was a dumb question, but I needed clarity.

Lydia's delicate shoulders tensed. "He's the only other Bellman in town. How do you know him?"

I needed to put her at ease. "I work at the diner, he came in for a cup of coffee this morning. He seems like a piece of work."

She cracked a small smile. "He definitely comes across as gruff, but he has a soft side. He can be very sweet. Only problem is he knows it, and uses it to his advantage. He's cocky in that sense." Her lower lip trembled. "I thought I could change him. Turn him from the player boy he was in high school into a loyal husband. But I guess some things never change."

I pulled her into a hug as tears began to fall from both our eyes. Hers because of her loss, and mine for knowing that someone else had to endure the same thing that caused me to leave my old life behind.

I broke from the hug and wiped the tears from my face. "What are you going to do with the mirror now?"

At that moment, Lydia stopped crying and wiped her eyes. She took a deep breath before speaking. "I don't want it. I only kept it because I'd thrown Jonah out before he had a chance to take it back."

I knew what I had to do. "Maybe I can take it off your hands? I know the owner of the store it came from, I'm sure she'll be happy to resell it."

Lydia looked relieved. "Thank you." her voice nearly squeaked.

"What will you do now then?

She shrugged. "I have a job and a house. That's all I really need."

"I mean what will you do about Jonah?"

Lydia's eyes filled with fear. "Keep my head low. He was mad when I rejected him the last time he came around." She pointed at the mirror in my hand. "He hasn't hurt me before, but after the death of his father, he's been different. More emotional. I'm afraid for whoever murdered his father. I've never seen him like that. I think he wants a shoulder to cry on, but I'm not ready to do that for him again." My heart ached for the girl.

Chapter 15

I returned to the antique shop with the gold mirror in my hands. I'd only been gone for about an hour, but when I got back, the mood had completely changed. When we'd first walked in, Nolan was clearly terrified of Vivi. But now, the two were talking and laughing like old friends as they polished a box of silverware.

"Hey, the traitor has returned." Nolan called as he waved a fork at me.

"Traitor? I was gone for only an hour."

Vivi finally looked up from the spoon in her hand. Her eyebrows were creased with worry.. "But where were you?"

I shrugged. "I was following a lead, and I found something." I set the mirror on the table and Vivi immediately stood up as if I'd been holding a bomb. "Where did you get that? Get it out of here." Her gentle, calm voice was now racked with disgust. Wait, no, not disgust, it was panic. Vivianne Thistle was scared. But why?

I reached for the mirror, but Vivi pulled my hand back. "Don't touch it. I'm surprised you made it here in one piece."

Now Nolan was confused as he stood up. "Is everything alright Miss Thistle?"

Vivi shook her head. "Why on earth would you bring a broken mirror into my store?"

"Because it's a clue-" I tried to explain.

"-it's not a clue, it's a disaster. Didn't your mother teach you anything?"

Nolan and I looked at each other even more confused. Vivi took a deep breath and managed to calm down a bit.

"Haven't either of you ever heard of the bylaw that a broken mirror-"

"-brings seven years of bad luck?" Nolan finished. I nodded in agreement.

"So you do know what I'm talking about. Then why would you be so careless?" Vivi turned to me with her eyes still blazing.

"Because it's just a superstition. It's not real." I felt annoyed at her making a big deal out of my clue.

Vivi walked over and slapped me across the face. I stumbled backwards and felt the burn of the slap on my face. Now I was really angry.

"What was that for? I'm trying to help you lady. This mirror was given to Lydia at the bank by her ex fiancee Jonah Bellman."

That stopped Vivi in her tracks. She looked down at the mirror on the table. "That is the same mirror I sold him, but I would never dare sell a broken mirror. That's bad news for everyone."

"Why? What's so bad about a broken mirror?" Now I was really curious.

The old woman removed her glasses and pinched the bridge of her nose. I felt bad for intruding, but there was something she was hiding. I had to know, and Nolan was feeling the same level of anticipation.

Vivi finally sat down, and as Nolan poured her another cup of tea, I urged her to talk.

"Very well." She finally gave in. "Many years ago, my grandparents immigrated to this country from England. They lived in a humble town that held a long history of myths and lore. They left for America because they hoped it would give them a better future free from persecution. Once they made it here, they began to build." As she spoke, Vivi's face became more wistful as she thought about old memories. "My grandfather was a carpenter, and he built all forms of exquisite furniture. Chairs, desks, even this very table that we are sitting at." I gasped softly and ran my hands over the polished wood.

"But it looks so new." I breathed.

Vivi nodded. "Grandpapa had a gift, and I don't mean he was skilled. He had a touch of magic that was passed down by the ancestors. His magic ensured that his work would never age, but instead, remain timeless forever."

"Magic? As in witchcraft?" I felt dread in my stomach.

The old woman nodded. "Magic. Witchcraft. Sorcery. It's been called many things. But regardless, it had existed for thousands of years in his hometown. But he and Grandmama left to get away from the mobs. They were ruthless pigs who wanted nothing more than to squash every last bit of magic out of England. My grandparents feared for their lives. So they bounced around the world until they came here and tried to keep his magic gift a secret from everyone."

"How did people react when they found out?" Nolan leaned in.

"They didn't. As far as they knew, he was gifted in carpentry. But they didn't realize just how big that gift was."

"So all of the items in here are infused with magic."
I glanced around the shop in awe.

Vivi shook her head. "Not everything." She took
another sip of tea before continuing.

"Back in England, my grandparents pulled their
magic from the roots of their magical town. They
had so many places and cities bathed in magic in
Europe that it was a special time, and so plentiful.
You could walk through a field of grass and feel the
power under your feet. Most of it came from nature,
but it was a fortuitous resource in their little town
especially. Lots of people used it for one reason or
another. Some were gifted in cooking and
gardening. Others were skilled in building and
weaving." She grabbed another cookie from the
plate. "Then things started to change when people
became scared of magic. The problem escalated to
an attempt to kill off anyone who practiced magic.
My grandparents left England before things got
really bad. They planned to continue using magic in
secret when they got to America. But when they got
there, they realized that America was not like
Europe at all."

"What was so different?" I wondered what could
change so drastically.

Vivi paused to gather her thoughts. "Contrary to
popular belief, magic itself is a very weak practice.
If I were to cast a simple spell to create fire, it would

take ten minutes for the flames to grow. Magic requires a little extra help to speed up the process."

"You mean like a catalyst?" Nolan's voice sounded excited.

"Exactly." Vivi began to talk faster as her excitement grew. "In the homeland there was magic, Grandpapa and the others used a soft mineral called Clyramarine. It was a blue gemstone that they would grind into a powder. When used in small doses, the powder would act as a catalyst to help to enhance their spells just enough and magic in the town. The spell did all the work, but the Clyramarine helped to speed up the magic process."

I frowned. "But what does that have to do with magic in America being different from magic in Europe?"

"Clyramarine is a rare mineral only found in England. Grandpapa moved here during the Gold Rush because he hoped that they would find Clyramarine too. They spent years trying to search for it in America, but there was none to be found. Later on, he tried to find a substitute, but it was no use. So Grandpapa spent the remainder of his days creating as many pieces of furniture as he could before he'd used up the last of the Clyramarine he had."

I raised my hand as if I was a child back in school. "Wait. But what does this have to do with the mirror?"

Another glance at the mirror caused Vivi to shudder again. "Once an object is infused with magic, it doesn't always stay there. It can spread and become infused into a different object. Magic itself is a curious thing. That mirror has been in this shop for years, I don't doubt it's absorbed at least a little bit of leftover magic. But it's not how the magic is absorbed, it's how it is dispersed from the object that can make it dangerous."

"Dangerous?" Nolan's voice tensed almost as fast as my heart.

"Dangerous." Vivi spoke with a low voice. "That superstition as you called it regarding seven years of bad luck when breaking a mirror is rooted in truth. If a magically infused object is damaged or cracked in any way, the magic leaks out the same way water would from a broken pipe. A little bit of magic is usually harmless. But when the magic is leaked out all at once, it can become dangerous. This is why I don't keep mirrors in the shop unless they can fit in the display case. Out of harm's way." Vivi pointed to the glass display case where she kept the jewelry collection.

"I still don't get it," Nolan took the words right out of my mouth.

Vivi sighed. "If an artifact is damaged in some way, the magic that was infused or absorbed into the object will be released. It will have to latch onto a host source or eventually die out. This can be any inanimate object. However, magic is more likely to latch onto a living being, like a plant, an animal, or even a human."

"What happens if it contacts a human?"

"If they have magical abilities, nothing. But for a non magic person, it can be jolting to their system. Almost like an electrical current passing through. Even if it is Pure Magic, a small amount will create a temporary shock, but an overwhelming amount of magic can be deadly. The end result can cause the body to shut down unexpectedly."

"Pure Magic?" Nolan looked confused.

"Pure Magic is any magic that hasn't been tainted through its use in spells. Any magic that's been used is often referred to as Dark Magic. Which is a bit of a misnomer. It's not necessarily bad, it's just not wise to reuse Dark Magic. It's harder to control, and usually contaminates the spell being cast. I don't like to take chances with Dark Magic infecting my store."

That caught my attention. "Vivi, do you think the mirror might be responsible for Mr. Bellman's death? Do you think that enough leaked magic could easily kill a human?"

Vivi shrugged. "It is very possible, but there's no way to prove it."

Nolan being the sensible one was the first to notice the flaw in our plan. "The police aren't going to accept this. They don't believe in magic, so there is no way that they will see this mirror as the murder suspect if it isn't already the weapon."

I knew Nolan and Vivi were right. Even if we could prove that the magic in the mirror had been used to kill Mr. Bellman, there was no way we could convince the police that Vivi hadn't infused the mirror with magic just to kill Mr. Bellman in the first place. There were a lot of what ifs.

"Wait!" I thought out loud. "Lydia said that Jonah had bought the mirror as a gift to her. She said he wanted to get back together. She didn't want to though. What if he broke the mirror and gave it to her out of anger."

Nolan shook his head. "How would he know there was magic in it?" He turned to Vivi. "Did Mr. Bellman know about the magic in your artifacts?"

I expected Vivi to shake her head, but she didn't. Instead, she nodded. "Mr. Bellman was aware of my family's history. He knew that magic was used by a select few to prolong the life of antique artifacts and furniture. However, it is a hard skill to sense magic embedded in objects. I was trained from a young age to detect traces of magic. But it took me years before I could do it effortlessly. He always came to me to verify his objects to ensure there wasn't any leftover Dark Magic left in anything. If there was, he asked me to remove it to prevent any accidents. He asked me to leave in just enough Pure Magic to preserve the artifacts, but not enough to cause problems."

We both saw where this was going. "Did Jonah know about this magic?" Nolan's shoulders began to tense, and I began to feel sick in my stomach.

Vivi shrugged. "I don't know. There is a chance, but hard to say for sure."

I stood up immediately. "Well whether or not he knows, I have a feeling he's still upset about his father's death."

Nolan stood up with me. "What are you doing now?" He looked more bored than annoyed.

I began walking toward the door. "If he knew about the mirror having magic in it, who was the one person he was most angry with? What if his father was an innocent bystander and not the target? What if that mirror wasn't a gift of love, but a gift of revenge."

Chapter 16

I silently kicked myself for not getting Lydia's number as I ran toward the bank. I checked my phone. It was almost five, so the bank hadn't closed just yet. What was I doing? How was I going to explain to Lydia that her ex had been trying to kill her with that mirror? Would she believe me, or would she think I was crazy? Even if I managed to protect her, how could I protect Vivi? There was no way that we could convince the police to arrest Jonah just because he'd given her a broken mirror? They would be laughing their heads off till next week.

As I reached the bank, I found Lydia getting into her car. Just as she was pulling out of the lot, I ran in front of her car and placed my hands up. I knew it was a stupid thing to do, but my body was surging with adrenaline, and I was panting as I climbed into the passenger seat.

Lydia was clearly furious. "Are you stalking me?"

I was about to open my mouth to explain, but she immediately began talking again. "No, don't talk, I don't want to know. Get out of my car right now or I will call the police." She pulled out her phone and opened a keypad to show she was serious.

I put my hands up in surrender. "Look, I'm sorry. I

really am. I wouldn't be here if I wasn't trying to protect you."

"Protect me? The only thing I need protecting from is you following me." Lydia placed a nine into the keypad, and began moving her finger toward the one. I felt time slipping through my own fingers.

"From your ex." That caused Lydia's head to snap up. "Excuse me?"

"Your ex? Jonah Bellman?" Lydia's face lit up when I said the name. "The mirror he gave you, it was filled with Dark Magic."

Now Lydia typed in one on the keypad. "Magic? Please, I may be young, but I'm not a child."

"The mirror was filled with Dark Magic. We think it was used to kill Richard Bellman. But I don't think he was the primary target. I think it was meant for-"

"We-" Lydia's face was now bright red. "What do you mean we? Are you working with the police? I don't see a badge…" her hand reached to press the final number on her phone.

On instinct, I reached over and snatched the phone. Now Lydia was really angry. She began to scream and reached over to grab the phone. I exited out of the call app, and turned off the phone.

"Look, I'm not trying to hurt you, but I need you to hear me out."

"I'm not hearing anything-"

"Look, listen to what I have to say, then you can call the police on me. Ok? I just need you to listen to me for a minute." With those words, Lydia finally stopped yelling. Her eyes were still red with rage, but she'd stopped trying to take the phone away from me, and that was a start.

I took a deep breath and counted to ten. "I'm not with the police. But I'm a friend of Vivianne Thistle from Thistle Antiques. We're trying to find the killer because if we don't the police will arrest her. She didn't do it. I know it. But they refuse to look for other suspects."

Lydia's shoulders relaxed just slightly, and I took a deep breath to continue. I told her about how we'd suspected Mr. Arched the first day we'd met. I then noted about Gregor's motive, and how that eventually led to meeting Jonah. That led to finding a connection between Jonah and the gold mirror, which led me to Lydia the second time. I explained how Vivi had a gift, and could suspect magic in older antiques. I left out the part that it was because she was a witch.

"Anyway, Vivi detected that there was a crack in the mirror, and that caused the magic that had been absorbed into the mirror to escape. All at once." I finally took a breath.

Lydia's eyebrows furrowed. "I still don't get it."

I nodded. "The magic that was in the mirror all escaped once it cracked. But Vivi said that once the magic is released, it latches onto the first living thing it finds. She said that if it latches onto a non magic being, it can feel like an electric shock. A fatal one."

Her dark eyes widened in recognition. "So what you're saying is that when the mirror broke, the magic released and was absorbed by Jonah's father? It wasn't a heart attack?" Her voice cracked as she mentioned her ex father in law.

"That's what it sounds like."

Lydia just sat there dumbfounded. She didn't move. I carefully handed her phone back, and she took it without turning her head.

Chapter 17

"So what do we do now?" Lydia's voice sounded on the verge of tears.

I shook my head. "I'm not sure. But I just thought you should know what we found."

"Why? What does this have to do with me?"

"Because I don't think that the Dark Magic in the mirror was intended for Mr. Bellman. I think he was an innocent bystander, and his heart attack was an accident. I think you were the target all along."

Her head snapped toward me. "Why me? Who would want me dead?"

"Didn't you say that your ex was mad because you refused to marry him?"

Realization dawned on Lydia's face, which was now pale white. "What should I do?"

I knew I couldn't leave her. I knew we needed to call the police, but I still was afraid to tell them about what we'd found.

"How about we go back to my place?" I offered. "You can stay the night, and tomorrow we'll go to the police."

"Why don't we just go right now? Wouldn't that be safer?" Lydia really looked scared now.

I shook my head. "There's no way they'll believe our story. A broken mirror murdering a man. They'll think we're crazy."

"What's going to change if we go tomorrow instead of today."

"I don't know. But maybe we can brainstorm and come up with an idea tonight. I don't know. It's all happening so fast. I need to think." I was starting to feel the reality of the situation.

Lydia seemed to agree with this idea. I called Nolan and told him to meet us at the diner in ten minutes. I figured if Jonah came wandering around, the two of us would be able to come up with a plan to convince the police to take us seriously.

On our way back to the diner, Lydia said she needed to pick something up at her house.

"Are you sure that's a good idea?" I asked. I just wanted to get home so I could lock all the doors forever. Or at least lock them until Nolan arrived with pizza.

"I need to feed my cat really fast."

"We can feed him tomorrow. RIght now we need to get to the diner. Nolan's meeting us there."

"I didn't have time to feed him this morning. I was late for a meeting and in a rush."

"Jonah knows where you live. He could be there right now."

That made Lydia drive faster. "If he's there right now, who knows what he might do to Earl."

"Earl? You named your cat Earl?" It wasn't my first choice for a cat name. Cats were supposed to have cute names like Pepper or Misty, not names stemmed from Nobility.

Lydia rolled her eyes as she pulled in front of an apartment building. "Long story. Just let me run inside and grab him. I'll be back in less than five minutes."

"Let me come with you." I unbuckled my seatbelt.

"No, he gets skittish around new people. It'll take longer. Just wait here."

I sighed reluctantly. "If you're not back in five minutes I'm coming up." I was warned.

Lydia nodded and ran up the stairs to her apartment.

I slowly counted the minutes. One minute. Two minutes. Three minutes. Once I hit the four minute mark, I got nervous. I felt my heart race. I counted down the last thirty seconds out loud to calm my nerves. Three, two, one. I jumped out of the car and ran up the stairs.

I knocked on the door. Nothing. I pounded on the door. Nothing. I grabbed the handle. unlocked. I burst into the apartment. The cool air brushed the hair from my face.

I took a few steps in and saw an old gray cat. I knelt down to pet him, but he ran away. I heard footsteps behind me, and just as I turned around, I saw a dark figure standing over me. Then everything went black.

Chapter 18

I felt my consciousness slowly return. Why did my head hurt? And why was it so cold? As I slowly opened my eyes, I saw the same gray cat. Earl I presume. Quite unfitting for a cat who did nothing more than hide and run. Where was the nobility in that?

I stretched lazily, but found my hands were bound. My hands behind my back with duct tape, and my feet to the legs of the chair I was sitting in. I glanced around the small kitchen and found Lydia taped to another chair in the middle of the room shaking. Standing in front of her was Jonah. Tears rolled down her face as she cried.

"Jonah please. You don't have to do this." she whimpered.

Jonah's face was hard and angry. "I don't have to do this?" he growled and jabbed her torso with the small handgun he held.. "You made me do this. You didn't have to break it off. We were in love. it's all your fault."

"My fault? You cheated on me. How did you expect me to handle that?"

"It was an accident. I didn't mean for it to happen."

"Didn't mean for it to happen? Or you didn't mean for me to find out?" Despite her fear, Lydia's voice was surprisingly calm in the moment. Almost as if she'd rehearsed for this moment.

Jonah's face turned red. At first I thought it was embarrassment, but when he pressed his gun into Lydia's left temple, I knew it was anger. Lydia closed her eyes and began to whimper. "I tried to be reasonable. I tried to be a good fiance. I was ready to leave my father so we could be together-"

"Wait." I shouted across the room. Both stared right at me. I knew I had a bump on my head the size of Texas, but that was no excuse for them to look at me as if I was a Maritan or something. I turned to the man holding the gun. "Jonah right? Hi, I don't believe we've met."

"I know you. You're that waitress chick. The one that kept listening in while I was talking to the detective."

I decided the truth was the best move right now. "Yep. And I think this whole thing is a complete misunderstanding." I was stalling, but I didn't have a choice.

Jonah lifted one eyebrow? "A misunderstanding huh? What part of this," he pointed between both of us in our chairs, "constitutes a misunderstanding?"

I felt my blood boil. "Hate to break it to you dude, but she's not coming back. You can plead and beg all you want, but she made the right move cutting you out.

Now I had his attention. "The right move? What makes you so sure of that?"

I shrugged. " Because I did the same thing with my ex. If he hadn't cheated on me, I wouldn't be here. Girls don't like guys who cheat on them, that's a fact."

Jonah scoffed. "And how is that working out for you? Working in a little diner in the middle of nowhere? Don't tell me that was your dream job."

I decided to say nothing. Let him keep talking. Maybe I'd find something I could use.

"I had everything. Did Lydia tell you we were set to be married next month? I was the happiest man on Earth. But I make one silly mistake, and everything falls apart."

"Oh don't give me that." Lydia growled. "You were sleeping with other women even before we got engaged. The only reason I said yes to marrying you was because you'd promised to not do it anymore. But when you broke your promise, things changed."

"I said I was sorry." Jonah's voice had an almost whine to it. He sounded like a child who'd never been told no before.

"But you broke my trust. I'm not going to spend my life with a man constantly chasing other women."

"Wait." I was desperate to keep them from fighting. "What are you going to do with us? You can't just kill us. Everyone will know it was you."

Jonah had a cold smile across his face. "It's quite simple really. She-" he pointed at Lydia. "-took everything from me. So I'm taking the one thing from here that means a lot to her."

"Money?" I asked stupidly.

Jonah slapped me across the face. That was two slaps in one day, and I did not appreciate it. He leaned in and met my eyes. "Freedom." that made my skin grow cold.

"How?" I whispered.

He smiled even bigger. "My father is dead. I can't do anything about that. But I can help the police find a killer."

"A killer?" I repeated stupidly. "They've already found one. They won't believe it was Lydia."

Jonah scoffed. "Yeah, I thought about that too. Vivianne and my father did business for years. I wanted to frame her initially. She's an easy target. But after Lydia rejected me a second time, I knew I had to get rid of her. I found my father on the floor after I brought her the mirror. At first I wanted to call an ambulance. I knew it was too late though. Must have been a heart attack. Then I realized it was the best way to get back at the girl who broke my heart."

"Frame her for murder? Oh how romantic."

Jonah sneered. "The old man was on death's door. I was prepared to hire a lawyer to help drop the charges. My lawyer in exchange for a second chance at marriage. But that went sideways when you got involved. I knew I had to kill her before the police traced everything back to me. Luckily, you're here too. Now we can tie up some loose ends." His voice was so calm, and I felt myself starting to panic.

Jonah cocked the handgun one more time, and looked between the two of us. He clearly decided he wanted to get rid of me first, and take his time with Lydia. I tried to keep my face calm, but I was scared.

His face was almost sympathetic now. "You should've just stayed with him. He could've provided for you. He made one simple mistake. Big deal. He's only human. What more do you expect from anyone?"

I felt my heart pound in my head. This was it. I was going to die. But at that moment, all I could think about was just how badly I'd left things with my mom. If I got out of this, I needed to patch things up. Sure we may have disagreed about Byron, but I didn't want it to separate us forever.

At that moment, I heard the door slam open. Officer Merrick and several other police officers ran in and aimed their guns at Jonah.

"Drop it now." Merrick shouted, his eyes narrowed into slits as he stepped toward Jonah.

"Lower your weapons or she dies." Jonah aimed the gun right at my head, and I closed my eyes.

"You don't have to do this Jonah, you're better than this."

At that moment, I knew how to solve all of my problems.

"Help me officer." I gave a high pitched cry. "He's going to kill me. Just like he killed his own father. Look, he's holding the weapon."

Jonah blanched. "What, no. I didn't kill my father, the guy had a heart attack. She's lying."

In his stupor, Jonah had lowered his gun from my head to my leg. Officer Merrick took that chance and shot the man in the chest. Jonah's body slumped against the wall, and all I could hear was Lydia's screams.

Chapter 19

Nolan ran to me as Officer Merrick helped me to the ambulance parked outside.

"Ivy? Are you ok? I heard the sirens?" His eyes were full of concern.

I was clearly in shock, but I wasn't hurt. I couldn't say the same for Jonah Bellman who was being carried out of the apartment in a bodybag. Lydia was off to the side with Chief Lawson, who was taking her statement. As Nolan covered me in a warm blanket, officer Merrick asked us to tell him everything.

Nolan helped me explain how we'd found the connection between Jonah and Lydia. We explained that Lydia had broken up with him because he'd cheated after they'd planned to run away from his father who didn't support their union. We decided to leave out all details about magic to ensure that Vivi was off the hook.

"So let me get this straight," Merrick looked up from his pad and pinched the bridge of his nose. "Jonah wanted to get back with Lydia, so his father gave him the idea to give her the antique mirror. Lydia didn't want to get back with him, which made him angry. So he killed his father with the letter opener out of rage?"

I shook my head. "No, he killed his father because he wanted to run away with Lydia. Gave him a heart attack using pills. Only problem was she didn't want him back. He killed his father before going to give Lydia the mirror, but when he got back, he knew he'd messed up. So instead of coming clean, he decided to blame Lydia for everything. He stabbed his own father with the letter opener to make it look like a murder."

Merrick shut his notebook. "That's messed up."

"You said it." Nolan agreed.

I began to cough, so Nolan ran to find me some water. Merrick was about to leave, but I grabbed his hand. It was warm compared to mine.

"Yes?" His green eyes looked worried.

I fumbled with the blanket as I walked over. I stared down at my shoes, and back up to his face. "Thank you." I mumbled.

His eyebrows furrowed. "What for?"

"For saving me. And for catching him." I pointed to the black body bag surrounded by officers.

He shrugged. "Just part of the job, I guess."

I reached up on my toes and planted a kiss on his cheek. "Thank you." He looked confused, but he didn't say anything as he turned around. I saw Nolan coming back and went to stand by the ambulance again.

Later that day, I decided to finally return the earrings to Vivi. Nolan demanded to go along with me.

"I am never leaving you out of my sight again." I rolled my eyes. "Not even while I sleep?"

Nolan paused. "Ok fine, but when you're in your apartment I know you're safe. But outside of there, I'm not leaving you."

"And the diner? Am I safe in the diner?" I smiled mischievously at him.

"Ok, the diner's fine, but anywhere else, I'm never letting you out of my sight. Not after what just happened."

The sky was streaked with gold from the sunset, and I felt the evening breeze blowing in.

As we made our way up the Victorian steps, Vivi greeted us both at the door with worry in her eyes. This time, she had a bright yellow sunflower brooch pinned to a white sweater.

"Goodness. I've been hearing the sirens for the past hour. Are you both alright?"

We glanced at one another. I still had a bump on my head and a headache, but I was alive. "We're ok." I told Vivi as she let us in and locked the door behind her.

Vivi handed us both steaming mugs of hot chocolate, which was some of the best I'd ever had. "So am I still a suspect?" Her eyes showed worry.

I shook my head. "No, the police blame Jonah Bellman for his father's death."

The old woman set her mug down. "Why would they do that? He didn't kill him, the mirror did."

Nolan grabbed a cookie off the tray, which warmed my heart. "Technically, he did bring the mirror into the house. He must have dropped it or something which caused the mirror to crack. So in that perspective, he did kill his father."

"But what about the letter opener?" Vivi and Nolan both turned to me.

I nodded. "Jonah said that when he got home, he thought his father had suffered a heart attack. I guess he didn't know about the magic in the mirror. But after his ex-fiancee rejected him, he wanted to blame her for all his problems. He tried to frame her by stabbing his own father with the letter opener to make it look like a murder."

Vivi rolled her eyes. "You can't blame another person for all of your problems. That's just going to cause pain for yourself."

I nodded in agreement. Then I remembered the reason for our visit, and pulled out the earrings from my pocket and handed them to Vivi.

Chapter 20

"Oh, you still have the earrings." Vivi's eyes sparkled. "Are you going to put them on?" She looked hopeful and I almost felt bad.

"No, I want to return them." That caused her face to fall, and I almost felt bad. "Don't get me wrong, they are very beautiful, just a little… um-"

"-Magic." Vivi finished for me. I nodded.

Vivi stood up and walked over to the cash register desk. She grabbed the same deep blue book with the strange silver markings she'd been reading when I first walked into the shop. When she opened it, I saw that it held drawings of different artifacts. A clock with a fish. A lamp covered in roses. Even a painting of a monkey in a suit.

"What's all this?" Nolan asked.

"This is my grandfather's grimoire. Now when most people think of a grimoire, they think of a book full of spells." She flipped through a few more pages. "This book holds a record of all of the magic artifacts he created in his life. After he passed, my parents continued to fill this book with pictures of magical artifacts they found in their lifetime. Including these." Viv pointed to a picture of earrings that looked exactly like the dragonfly ones I was holding.

"What does it say? Nolan's eyes were huge, I thought they would explode.

"It says here that dragonflies are a symbol of change and transformation. The earrings are believed to glow when something big changes in someone's life."

"Just like in the restaurant?" I breathed. They glowed at the same time that Mr. Bellman had died.

Vivi nodded. "Exactly. They serve as a guide when something happens. They encourage you to be ready to take initiative when this change does happen. Sort of a wake up call if you know what I mean."

I nodded slowly. The earrings in my hands didn't feel so heavy anymore. "You know what?" I said to Vivi. "I think I'm going to hold onto these for just a little longer." I put the earrings on, and turned to smile at my reflection in the mirror.

The old woman smiled. "I'm glad. They do look lovely on you."

"She's right, you know." Nolan agreed, and I smiled even more.

Vivi then stood up from the table. "Well I think you two better go home. You've had a long day, and so have I. I'm an old woman, and I need my beauty sleep." Nolan and I smiled at that last comment. "But I expect to see you both tomorrow night." "Tomorrow night?" Nolan and I exchanged looks.

Vivi paused and turned around. "I thought maybe you both would want to know more about the magic in this shop. Besides, I need two apprentices to help me burn that." She pointed to the broken mirror, which was now on the floor sitting inside a ring of salt, herbs, and crystals.

"Burn it?" I asked.

"Yes. You have to burn an object filled with Dark Magic, otherwise it'll just keep on absorbing and leaking it. It's a dangerous thing to just have lying around. Better to burn it before it can do any more harm."

I wanted to protest, but Nolan put a hand on my shoulder. "We'll be there tomorrow Vivi."

"You better be. It has to be done on a full moon, which is tomorrow. I'm not waiting until next month just because you two can't appreciate the fine art of-"

"We'll be there Vivi. I promise." I wasn't in the mood for a lecture, and I needed to get back to my apartment.

Vivi nodded and went up the stairs to her room. Nolan drove me back, and dropped me off without a word.

I slowly trudged up the steps to my apartment, and collapsed onto my bed. It really had been a long day, but it was over. I didn't want to leave home for ages.

Home. I'd only been in Redwood Bluff for a few short days, but I already felt at home. I had a job, an apartment, and most all, I had friends. That idea warmed my heart. I'd nearly forgotten about my ex, which was fine because if he'd wanted me back, he would've at least called.

Then I remembered mom. I didn't want it to end like this. If anything, Jonah made me realize how much I valued family. I didn't want our relationship to fail just because I was angry at her. I needed to fix this. I reached for the phone. She was going to be mad, it was going to hurt. I took a deep breath. But I needed her to understand that I was happy. Yes I was working in a diner, and I didn't have a man, but I was happier here. She would have to accept that. At least for now. I thought about officer Merrick and how he'd saved me. Those green eyes were hard to forget.

I pressed the call button on my phone. On the other line, I heard my mother's airy hello.

About the Author

Alyssa Brown is an artist and a graphic designer with a passion for writing. From a young age, she developed a love for storytelling, and spent at least half of her life reading new stories and writing her own. Alyssa is a student at Brigham Young University in Provo, Utah focusing on arts and design. She is becoming an artist and with the release of this book has become a first time author.